Lizzie Leigh

Elizabeth Gaskell

CHAPTER I.

When Death is present in a household on a Christmas Day, the very contrast between the time as it now is, and the day as it has often been, gives a poignancy to sorrow--a more utter blankness to the desolation. James Leigh died just as the far-away bells of Rochdale Church were ringing for morning service on Christmas Day, 1836. A few minutes before his death, he opened his already glazing eyes, and made a sign to his wife, by the faint motion of his lips, that he had yet something to say. She stooped close down, and caught the broken whisper, "I forgive her, Annie! May God forgive me!"

Regret

"Oh, my love, my dear! only get well, and I will never cease showing my thanks for those words. May God in heaven bless thee for saying them. Thou'rt not so restless, my lad! may be--Oh, God!"

For even while she spoke he died.

They had been two-and-twenty years man and wife; for nineteen of those years their life had been as calm and happy as the most perfect uprightness on the one side, and the most complete confidence and loving submission on the other, could make it. Milton's famous line might have been framed and hung up as the rule of their married life, for he was truly the interpreter, who stood between God and her; she would have considered herself wicked if she had ever dared even to think him austere, though as certainly as he was an upright man, so surely was he hard, stern, and inflexible. But for three years the moan and the murmur had never been out of her heart; she had rebelled against her husband as against a tyrant, with a hidden, sullen rebellion, which tore up the old landmarks of wifely duty and affection, and poisoned the fountains whence gentlest love and reverence had once been for ever springing.

wife feeling towards husband.

But those last blessed words replaced him on his throne in her heart, and called out penitent anguish for all the bitter estrangement of later years. It was this which made her refuse all the entreaties of her sons, that she would see the kind-hearted neighbours, who called on their way from church, to sympathize and condole. No! she would stay with the dead husband that had spoken tenderly at last, if for three years he had kept silence; who knew but what, if she had only been more gentle and less angrily reserved he might have relented earlier--and in time?

She sat rocking herself to and fro by the side of the bed, while the footsteps below went in and out; she had been in sorrow too long to have any violent burst of deep grief now; the furrows were well worn in her cheeks, and the tears flowed quietly, if incessantly, all the day long. But when the winter's night drew on, and the neighbours had gone away to their homes, she stole to the window, and gazed out, long and wistfully, over the dark grey moors. She did not hear her son's voice, as he spoke to her from the door, nor his footstep as he drew nearer. She started when he touched her.

"Mother! come down to us. There's no one but Will and me. Dearest mother, we do so want you." The poor lad's voice trembled, and he began to cry. It appeared to require an effort on Mrs. Leigh's part to tear herself away from the window, but with a sigh she complied with his request.

The two boys (for though Will was nearly twenty-one, she still thought of him as a lad) had done everything in their power to make the house-place comfortable for her. She herself, in the old days before her sorrow, had never made a brighter fire or a cleaner hearth, ready for her husband's return home, than now awaited her. The tea-things were all put out, and the kettle was boiling; and the boys had calmed their grief down into a kind of sober cheerfulness. They paid her every attention they could think of, but received little notice on her part; she did not resist, she rather submitted to all their arrangements; but they did not seem to touch her heart.

When tea was ended--it was merely the form of tea that had been gone through--Will moved the things away to the dresser. His mother leant back languidly in her chair.

"Mother, shall Tom read you a chapter? He's a better scholar than I."

"Ay, lad!" said she, almost eagerly. "That's it. Read me the Prodigal Son. Ay, ay, lad. Thank thee."

Tom found the chapter, and read it in the high-pitched voice which is customary in village schools. His mother bent forward, her lips parted, her eyes dilated; her whole body instinct with eager attention. Will sat with his head depressed and hung down. He knew why that chapter had been chosen; and to him it recalled the family's disgrace. When the reading was ended, he still hung down his head in gloomy silence. But her face was brighter than it had been before for the day. Her eyes looked dreamy, as if she saw a vision; and by- and-by she pulled the Bible towards her, and, putting her finger underneath each word, began to read them aloud in a low voice to herself; she read again the words of bitter sorrow and deep humiliation; but most of all, she paused and brightened over the father's tender reception of the repentant prodigal.

So passed the Christmas evening in the Upclose Farm.

The snow had fallen heavily over the dark waving moorland before the day of the funeral. The black storm-laden dome of heaven lay very still and close upon the white earth, as they carried the body forth out of the house which had known his presence so long as its ruling power. Two and two the mourners followed, making a black procession, in their winding march over the unbeaten snow, to Milne Row Church; now lost in some hollow of the bleak moors, now slowly climbing the heaving ascents. There was no long tarrying after the funeral, for many of the neighbours who accompanied the body to the grave had far to go, and the great white flakes which came slowly down were the boding forerunners of a heavy storm. One old friend alone accompanied the widow and her sons to their home.

The Upclose Farm had belonged for generations to the Leighs; and yet its possession hardly raised them above the rank of labourers. There was the house and out-buildings, all of an old-fashioned kind, and about seven acres of barren unproductive land, which they had never possessed capital enough to improve; indeed, they could hardly rely upon it for subsistence; and it had been customary to bring up the sons to some trade, such as a wheelwright's or blacksmith's.

James Leigh had left a will in the possession of the old man who accompanied them home. He read it aloud. James had bequeathed the farm to his faithful wife, Anne Leigh, for her lifetime, and afterwards to his son William. The hundred and odd pounds in the savings bank was to accumulate for Thomas.

iv

After the reading was ended, Anne Leigh sat silent for a time and then she asked to speak to Samuel Orme alone. The sons went into the back kitchen, and thence strolled out into the fields regardless of the driving snow. The brothers were dearly fond of each other, although they were very different in character. Will, the elder, was like his father, stern, reserved, and scrupulously upright. Tom (who was ten years younger) was gentle and delicate as a girl, both in appearance and character. He had always clung to his mother arid dreaded his father. They did not speak as they walked, for they were only in the habit of talking about facts, and hardly knew the more sophisticated language applied to the description of feelings.

Meanwhile their mother had taken hold of Samuel Orme's arm with her trembling hand.

"Samuel, I must let the farm--I must."

"Let the farm! What's come o'er the woman?"

"Oh, Samuel!" said she, her eyes swimming in tears, "I'm just fain to go and live in Manchester. I mun let the farm."

Samuel looked, and pondered, but did not speak for some time. At last he said -

"If thou hast made up thy mind, there's no speaking again it; and thou must e'en go. Thou'lt be sadly pottered wi' Manchester ways; but that's not my look out. Why, thou'lt have to buy potatoes, a thing thou hast never done afore in all thy born life. Well! it's not my look out. It's rather for me than again me. Our Jenny is going to be married to Tom Higginbotham, and he was speaking of wanting a bit of land to begin upon. His father will be dying sometime, I reckon, and then he'll step into the Croft Farm. But meanwhile--"

"Then, thou'lt let the farm," said she, still as eagerly as ever.

"Ay, ay, he'll take it fast enough, I've a notion. But I'll not drive a bargain with thee just now; it would not be right; we'll wait a bit."

"No; I cannot wait; settle it out at once."

"Well, well; I'll speak to Will about it. I see him out yonder. I'll step to him and talk it over."

v

Accordingly he went and joined the two lads, and, without more ado, began the subject to them.

"Will, thy mother is fain to go live in Manchester, and covets to let the farm. Now, I'm willing to take it for Tom Higginbotham; but I like to drive a keen bargain, and there would be no fun chaffering with thy mother just now. Let thee and me buckle to, my lad! and try and cheat each other; it will warm us this cold day."

"Let the farm!" said both the lads at once, with infinite surprise. "Go live in Manchester!"

When Samuel Orme found that the plan had never before been named to either Will or Tom, he would have nothing to do with it, he said, until they had spoken to their mother. Likely she was "dazed" by her husband's death; he would wait a day or two, and not name it to any one; not to Tom Higginbotham himself, or may be he would set his heart upon it. The lads had better go in and talk it over with their mother. He bade them good-day, and left them.

Will looked very gloomy, but he did not speak till they got near the house. Then he said -

"Tom, go to th' shippon, and supper the cows. I want to speak to mother alone."

When he entered the house-place, she was sitting before the fire, looking into its embers. She did not hear him come in: for some time she had lost her quick perception of outward things.

"Mother! what's this about going to Manchester?" asked he.

"Oh, lad!" said she, turning round, and speaking in a beseeching tone, "I must go and seek our Lizzie. I cannot rest here for thinking on her. Many's the time I've left thy father sleeping in bed, and stole to th' window, and looked and looked my heart out towards Manchester, till I thought I must just set out and tramp over moor and moss straight away till I got there, and then lift up every downcast face till I came to our Lizzie. And often, when the south wind was blowing soft among the hollows, I've fancied (it could but be fancy, thou knowest) I heard her crying upon me; and I've thought the voice came closer and closer, till at last it was sobbing out, 'Mother!' close to the door; and I've stolen down, and undone the latch before now, and looked out into the still, black night, thinking to see her--and turned sick and sorrowful when I heard no living sound but the sough of the wind dying away. Oh, speak not to me of stopping here, when she may be perishing for hunger, like the poor lad in the parable." And now she lifted up her voice, and wept aloud.

Will was deeply grieved. He had been old enough to be told the family shame when, more than two years before, his father had had his letter to his daughter returned by her mistress in Manchester, telling him that Lizzie had left her service some time--and why. He had sympathized with his father's stern anger; though he had thought him something hard, it is true, when he had forbidden his weeping, heart-broken wife to go and try to find her poor sinning child, and declared that henceforth they would have no daughter; that she should be as one dead, and her name never more be named at market or at meal time, in blessing or in prayer. He had held his peace, with compressed lips and contracted brow, when the neighbours had noticed to him how poor Lizzie's death had aged both his father and his mother; and how they thought the bereaved couple would never hold up their heads again. He himself had felt as if that one event had made him old before his time; and had envied Tom the tears he had shed over poor, pretty, innocent, dead Lizzie. He thought about her sometimes, till he ground his teeth together, and could have struck her down in her shame. His mother had never named her to him until now.

"Mother!" said he, at last. "She may be dead. Most likely she is"

"No, Will; she is not dead," said Mrs. Leigh. "God will not let her die till I've seen her once again. Thou dost not know how I've prayed and prayed just once again to see her sweet face, and tell her I've forgiven her, though she's broken my heart--she has, Will." She could not go on for a minute or two for the choking sobs. "Thou dost not know that, or thou wouldst not say she could be dead--for God is very merciful, Will; He is: He is much more pitiful than man. I could never ha' spoken to thy father as I did to Him--and yet thy father forgave her at last. The last words he said were that he forgave her. Thou'lt not be harder than thy father, Will? Do not try and hinder me going to seek her, for it's no use."

Will sat very still for a long time before he spoke. At last he said, "I'll not hinder you. I think she's dead, but that's no matter."

"She's not dead," said her mother, with low earnestness. Will took no notice of the interruption.

"We will all go to Manchester for a twelvemonth, and let the farm to Tom Higginbotham. I'll get blacksmith's work; and Tom can have good schooling for awhile, which he's always craving for. At the end of the year you'll come back, mother, and give over fretting for Lizzie, and think with me that she is dead--and, to my mind, that would be more comfort than to think of her living;" he dropped his voice as he spoke these last words. She shook her head but made no answer. He asked again--"Will you, mother, agree to this?"

"I'll agree to it a-this-ns," said she. "If I hear and see nought of her for a twelvemonth, me being in Manchester looking out, I'll just ha' broken my heart fairly before the year's ended, and then I shall know neither love nor sorrow for her any more, when I'm at rest in my grave. I'll agree to that, Will."

"Well, I suppose it must be so. I shall not tell Tom, mother, why we're flitting to Manchester. Best spare him."

"As thou wilt," said she, sadly, "so that we go, that's all."

Before the wild daffodils were in flower in the sheltered copses round Upclose Farm, the Leighs were settled in their Manchester home; if they could ever grow to consider that place as a home, where there was no garden or outbuilding, no fresh breezy outlet, no far- stretching view, over moor and hollow; no dumb animals to be tended, and, what more than all they missed, no old haunting memories, even though those remembrances told of sorrow, and the dead and gone.

Mrs. Leigh heeded the loss of all these things less than her sons. She had more spirit in her countenance than she had had for months, because now she had hope; of a sad enough kind, to be sure, but still it was hope. She performed all her household duties, strange and complicated as they were, and bewildered as she was with all the town necessities of her new manner of life; but when her house was "sided," and the boys come home from their work in the evening, she would put on her things and steal out, unnoticed, as she thought, but not without many a heavy sigh from Will, after she had closed the house-door and departed. It was often past midnight before she came back, pale and weary, with almost a guilty look upon her face; but that face so full of disappointment and hope deferred, that Will had never the heart to say what he thought of the folly and hopelessness of the search. Night after night it was renewed, till days grew to weeks, and weeks to months. All this time Will did his duty towards her as well as he could, without having sympathy with her. He stayed at home in the evenings for Tom's sake, and often wished he had Tom's pleasure in reading, for the time hung heavy on his hands as he sat up for his mother.

I need not tell you how the mother spent the weary hours. And yet I will tell you something. She used to wander out, at first as if without a purpose, till she rallied her thoughts, and brought all her energies to bear on the one point; then she went with earnest patience along the least-known ways to some new part of the town, looking wistfully with dumb entreaty into people's faces; sometimes catching a glimpse of a figure which had a kind of momentary likeness to her child's, and following that figure with never-wearying perseverance, till some light from shop or lamp showed the cold strange face which was not her daughter's. Once or twice a kind- hearted passer-by, struck by her look of yearning woe, turned back and offered help, or asked her what she wanted. When so spoken to, she answered only, "You don't know a poor girl they call Lizzie Leigh, do you?" and when they denied all knowledge, she shook her head, and went on again. I think they believed her to be crazy. But she never spoke first to any one. She sometimes took a few minutes' rest on the door-steps, and sometimes (very seldom) covered her face and cried; but she could not afford to lose time and chances in this way; while her eyes were blinded with tears, the lost one might pass by unseen.

One evening, in the rich time of shortening autumn-days, Will saw an old man, who, without being absolutely drunk, could not guide himself rightly along the foot-path, and was mocked for his unsteadiness of gait by the idle boys of the neighbourhood. For his father's sake, Will regarded old age with tenderness, even when most degraded and removed from the stern virtues which dignified that father; so he took the old man home, and seemed to believe his often-repeated assertions, that he drank nothing but water. The stranger tried to stiffen himself up into steadiness as he drew nearer home, as if there some one there for whose respect he cared even in his half- intoxicated state, or whose feelings he feared to grieve. His home was exquisitely clean and neat, even in outside appearance; threshold, window, and windowsill were outward signs of some spirit of purity within. Will was rewarded for his attention by a bright glance of thanks, succeeded by a blush of shame, from a young woman of twenty or thereabouts. She did not speak or second her father's hospitable invitations to him to be seated. She seemed unwilling that a stranger should witness her father's attempts at stately sobriety, and Will could not bear to stay and see her distress. But when the old man, with many a flabby shake of the hand, kept asking him to come again some other evening, and see them, Will sought her downcast eyes, and, though he could not read their veiled meaning, he answered, timidly, "If it's agreeable to everybody, I'll come, and thank ye." But there was no answer from the girl, to whom this speech was in reality addressed; and Will left the house, liking her all the better for never speaking.

He thought about her a great deal for the next day or two; he scolded himself for being so foolish as to think of her, and then fell to with fresh vigour, and thought of her more than ever. He tried to depreciate her: he told himself she was not pretty, and then made indignant answer that he liked her looks much better than any beauty of them all. He wished he was not so country-looking, so red-faced, so broad-shouldered; while she was like a lady, with her smooth, colourless complexion, her bright dark hair, and her spotless dress. Pretty or not pretty she drew his footsteps towards her; he could not resist the impulse that made him wish to see her once more, and find out some fault which should unloose his heart from her unconscious keeping. But there she was, pure and maidenly as before. He sat and looked, answering her father at cross-purposes, while she drew more and more into the shadow of the chimney-corner out of sight. Then the spirit that possessed him (it was not he himself, sure, that did so impudent a thing!) made him get up and carry the candle to a different place, under the pretence of giving her more light at her sewing, but in reality to be able to see her better. She could not stand this much longer, but jumped up and said she must put her little niece to bed; and surely there never was, before or since, so troublesome a child of two years old, for though Will stayed an hour and a half longer, she never came down again. He won the father's heart, though, by his capacity as a listener; for some people are not at all particular, and, so that they themselves may talk on undisturbed, are not so unreasonable as to expect attention to what they say.

Will did gather this much, however, from the old man's talk. He had once been quite in a genteel line of business, but had failed for more money than any greengrocer he had heard of; at least, any who did not mix up fish and game with green-grocery proper. This grand failure seemed to have been the event of his life, and one on which he dwelt with a strange kind of pride. It appeared as if at present he rested from his past exertions (in the bankrupt line), and depended on his daughter, who kept a small school for very young children. But all these particulars Will only remembered and understood when he had left the house; at the time he heard them, he was thinking of Susan. After he had made good his footing at Mr. Palmer's, he was not long, you may be sure, without finding some reason for returning again and again. He listened to her father, he talked to the little niece, but he looked at Susan, both while he listened and while he talked. Her father kept on insisting upon his former gentility, the details of which would have appeared very questionable to Will's mind, if the sweet, delicate, modest Susan had not thrown an inexplicable air of refinement over all she came near. She never spoke much; she was generally diligently at work; but when she moved it was so noiselessly, and when she did speak, it was in so low and soft a voice, that silence, speech, motion, and stillness alike seemed to remove her high above Will's reach into some saintly and inaccessible air of glory--high above his reach, even as she knew him! And, if she were made acquainted with the dark secret behind of his sister's shame, which was kept ever present to his mind by his mother's nightly search among the outcast and forsaken, would not Susan shrink away from him with loathing, as if he were tainted by the involuntary relationship? This was his dread; and thereupon followed a resolution that he would withdraw from her sweet company before it was too late. So he resisted internal temptation, and stayed at home, and suffered and sighed. He became angry with his mother for her untiring patience in seeking for one who he could not help hoping was dead rather than alive. He spoke sharply to her, and received only such sad deprecatory answers as made him reproach himself, and still more lose sight of peace of mind. This struggle could not last long without affecting his health; and Tom, his sole companion through the long evenings, noticed his increasing languor, his restless irritability, with perplexed anxiety, and at last resolved to call his mother's attention to his brother's haggard, careworn looks. She listened with a startled recollection of Will's claims upon her love. She noticed his decreasing appetite and half- checked sighs.

"Will, lad! what's come o'er thee?" said she to him, as he sat listlessly gazing into the fire.

"There's nought the matter with me," said he, as if annoyed at her remark.

"Nay, lad, but there is." He did not speak again to contradict her; indeed, she did not know if he had heard her, so unmoved did he look.

"Wouldst like to go to Upclose Farm?" asked she, sorrowfully.

"It's just blackberrying time," said Tom.

Will shook his head. She looked at him awhile, as if trying to read that expression of despondency, and trace it back to its source.

"Will and Tom could go," said she; "I must stay here till I've found her, thou knowest," continued she, dropping her voice.

He turned quickly round, and with the authority he at all times exercised over Tom, bade him begone to bed.

When Tom had left the room, he prepared to speak.

CHAPTER II.

"Mother," then said Will, "why will you keep on thinking she's alive? If she were but dead, we need never name her name again. We've never heard nought on her since father wrote her that letter; we never knew whether she got it or not. She'd left her place before then. Many a one dies in--"

"Oh, my lad! dunnot speak so to me, or my heart will break outright," said his mother, with a sort of cry. Then she calmed herself, for she yearned to persuade him to her own belief. "Thou never asked, and thou'rt too like thy father for me to tell without asking--but it were all to be near Lizzie's old place that I settled down on this side o' Manchester; and the very day at after we came, I went to her old missus, and asked to speak a word wi' her. I had a strong mind to cast it up to her, that she should ha' sent my poor lass away, without telling on it to us first; but she were in black, and looked so sad I could na' find in my heart to threep it up. But I did ask her a bit about our Lizzie. The master would have turned her away at a day's warning (he's gone to t'other place; I hope he'll meet wi' more mercy there than he showed our Lizzie--I do), and when the missus asked her should she write to us, she says Lizzie shook her head; and when she speered at her again, the poor lass went down on her knees, and begged her not, for she said it would break my heart (as it has done, Will--God knows it has)," said the poor mother, choking with her struggle to keep down her hard overmastering grief, "and her father would curse her--Oh, God, teach me to be patient." She could not speak for a few minutes--"and the lass threatened, and said she'd go drown herself in the canal, if the missus wrote home-- and so -

"Well! I'd got a trace of my child--the missus thought she'd gone to th' workhouse to be nursed; and there I went--and there, sure enough, she had been--and they'd turned her out as she were strong, and told her she were young enough to work--but whatten kind o' work would be open to her, lad, and her baby to keep?"

Will listened to his mother's tale with deep sympathy, not unmixed with the old bitter shame. But the opening of her heart had unlocked his, and after awhile he spoke -

"Mother! I think I'd e'en better go home. Tom can stay wi' thee. I know I should stay too, but I cannot stay in peace so near--her-- without craving to see her--Susan Palmer, I mean."

"Has the old Mr. Palmer thou telled me on a daughter?" asked Mrs. Leigh.

"Ay, he has. And I love her above a bit. And it's because I love her I want to leave Manchester. That's all."

Mrs. Leigh tried to understand this speech for some time, but found it difficult of interpretation.

"Why shouldst thou not tell her thou lov'st her? Thou'rt a likely lad, and sure o' work. Thou'lt have Upclose at my death; and as for that, I could let thee have it now, and keep mysel' by doing a bit of charring. It seems to me a very backwards sort o' way of winning her to think of leaving Manchester."

"Oh, mother, she's so gentle and so good--she's downright holy. She's never known a touch of sin; and can I ask her to marry me, knowing what we do about Lizzie, and fearing worse? I doubt if one like her could ever care for me; but if she knew about my sister, it would put a gulf between us, and she'd shudder up at the thought of crossing it. You don't know how good she is, mother!"

"Will, Will! if she's so good as thou say'st, she'll have pity on such as my Lizzie. If she has no pity for such, she's a cruel Pharisee, and thou'rt best without her."

But he only shook his head, and sighed; and for the time the conversation dropped.

But a new idea sprang up in Mrs. Leigh's head. She thought that she would go and see Susan Palmer, and speak up for Will, and tell her the truth about Lizzie; and according to her pity for the poor sinner, would she be worthy or unworthy of him. She resolved to go the very next afternoon, but without telling any one of her plan. Accordingly she looked out the Sunday clothes she had never before had the heart to unpack since she came to Manchester, but which she now desired to appear in, in order to do credit to Will. She put on her old-fashioned black mode bonnet, trimmed with real lace; her scarlet cloth cloak, which she had had ever since she was married; and, always spotlessly clean, she set forth on her unauthorised embassy. She knew the Palmers lived in Crown Street, though where she had heard it she could not tell; and modestly asking her way, she arrived in the street about a quarter to four o'clock. She stopped to enquire the exact number, and the woman whom she addressed told her that Susan Palmer's school would not be loosed till four, and asked her to step in and wait until then at her house.

"For," said she, smiling, "them that wants Susan Palmer wants a kind friend of ours; so we, in a manner, call cousins. Sit down, missus, sit down. I'll wipe the chair, so that it shanna dirty your cloak. My mother used to wear them bright cloaks, and they're right gradely things again a green field."

"Han ye known Susan Palmer long?" asked Mrs. Leigh, pleased with the admiration of her cloak.

"Ever since they comed to live in our street. Our Sally goes to her school."

"Whatten sort of a lass is she, for I ha' never seen her?"

"Well, as for looks, I cannot say. It's so long since I first knowed her, that I've clean forgotten what I thought of her then. My master says he never saw such a smile for gladdening the heart. But maybe it's not looks you're asking about. The best thing I can say of her looks is, that she's just one a stranger would stop in the street to ask help from if he needed it. All the little childer creeps as close as they can to her; she'll have as many as three or four hanging to her apron all at once."

"Is she cocket at all?"

"Cocket, bless you! you never saw a creature less set up in all your life. Her father's cocket enough. No! she's not cocket any way. You've not heard much of Susan Palmer, I reckon, if you think she's cocket. She's just one to come quietly in, and do the very thing most wanted; little things, maybe, that any one could do, but that few would think on, for another. She'll bring her thimble wi' her, and mend up after the childer o' nights; and she writes all Betty Harker's letters to her grandchild out at service; and she's in nobody's way, and that's a great matter, I take it. Here's the childer running past! School is loosed. You'll find her now, missus, ready to hear and to help. But we none on us frab her by going near her in school-time."

Poor Mrs. Leigh's heart began to beat, and she could almost have turned round and gone home again. Her country breeding had made her shy of strangers, and this Susan Palmer appeared to her like a real born lady by all accounts. So she knocked with a timid feeling at the indicated door, and when it was opened, dropped a simple curtsey without speaking. Susan had her little niece in her arms, curled up with fond endearment against her breast, but she put her gently down to the ground, and instantly placed a chair in the best corner of the room for Mrs. Leigh, when she told her who she was. "It's not Will as has asked me to come," said the mother, apologetically; "I'd a wish just to speak to you myself!"

Susan coloured up to her temples, and stooped to pick up the little toddling girl. In a minute or two Mrs. Leigh began again.

"Will thinks you would na respect us if you knew all; but I think you could na help feeling for us in the sorrow God has put upon us; so I just put on my bonnet, and came off unknownst to the lads. Every one says you're very good, and that the Lord has keeped you from falling from His ways; but maybe you've never yet been tried and tempted as some is. I'm perhaps speaking too plain, but my heart's welly broken, and I can't be choice in my words as them who are happy can. Well now! I'll tell you the truth. Will dreads you to hear it, but I'll just tell it you. You mun know--" but here the poor woman's words failed her, and she could do nothing but sit rocking herself backwards and forwards, with sad eyes, straight-gazing into Susan's face, as if they tried to tell the tale of agony which the quivering lips refused to utter. Those wretched, stony eyes forced the tears down Susan's cheeks, and, as if this sympathy gave the mother strength, she went on in a low voice--"I had a daughter once, my heart's darling. Her father thought I made too much on her, and that she'd grow marred staying at home; so he said she mun go among strangers and learn to rough it. She were young, and liked the thought of seeing a bit of the world; and her father heard on a place in Manchester. Well! I'll not weary you. That poor girl were led astray; and first thing we heard on it, was when a letter of her father's was sent back by her missus, saying she'd left her place, or, to speak right, the master had turned her into the street soon as he had heard of her condition--and she not seventeen!"

She now cried aloud; and Susan wept too. The little child looked up into their faces, and, catching their sorrow, began to whimper and wail. Susan took it softly up, and hiding her face in its little neck, tried to restrain her tears, and think of comfort for the mother. At last she said -

"Where is she now?"

"Lass! I dunnot know," said Mrs. Leigh, checking her sobs to communicate this addition to her distress. "Mrs. Lomax telled me she went--"

"Mrs. Lomax--what Mrs. Lomax?"

"Her as lives in Brabazon Street. She told me my poor wench went to the workhouse fra there. I'll not speak again the dead; but if her father would but ha' letten me--but he were one who had no notion--no, I'll not say that; best say nought. He forgave her on his death-bed. I daresay I did na go th' right way to work."

"Will you hold the child for me one instant?" said Susan.

"Ay, if it will come to me. Childer used to be fond on me till I got the sad look on my face that scares them, I think."

But the little girl clung to Susan; so she carried it upstairs with her. Mrs. Leigh sat by herself--how long she did not know.

Susan came down with a bundle of far-worn baby-clothes.

"You must listen to me a bit, and not think too much about what I'm going to tell you. Nanny is not my niece, nor any kin to me, that I know of. I used to go out working by the day. One night, as I came home, I thought some woman was following me; I turned to look. The woman, before I could see her face (for she turned it to one side), offered me something. I held out my arms by instinct; she dropped a bundle into them, with a bursting sob that went straight to my heart. It was a baby. I looked round again; but the woman was gone. She had run away as quick as lightning. There was a little packet of clothes--very few--and as if they were made out of its mother's gowns, for they were large patterns to buy for a baby. I was always fond of babies; and I had not my wits about me, father says; for it was very cold, and when I'd seen as well as I could (for it was past ten) that there was no one in the street, I brought it in and warmed it. Father was very angry when he came, and said he'd take it to the workhouse the next morning, and flyted me sadly about it. But when morning came I could not bear to part with it; it had slept in my arms all night; and I've heard what workhouse bringing-up is. So I told father I'd give up going out working and stay at home and keep school, if I might only keep the baby; and, after a while, he said if I earned enough for him to have his comforts, he'd let me; but he's never taken to her. Now, don't tremble so--I've but a little more to tell--and maybe I'm wrong in telling it; but I used to work next door to Mrs. Lomax's, in Brabazon Street, and the servants were all thick together; and I heard about Bessy (they called her) being sent away. I don't know that ever I saw her; but the time would be about fitting to this child's age, and I've sometimes fancied it was hers. And now, will you look at the little clothes that came with her--bless her!"

But Mrs. Leigh had fainted. The strange joy and shame, and gushing love for the little child, had overpowered her; it was some time before Susan could bring her round. There she was all trembling, sick with impatience to look at the little frocks. Among them was a slip of paper which Susan had forgotten to name, that had been pinned to the bundle. On it was scrawled in a round stiff hand -

"Call her Anne. She does not cry much, and takes a deal of notice. God bless you and forgive me."

The writing was no clue at all; the name "Anne," common though it was, seemed something to build upon. But Mrs. Leigh recognised one of the frocks instantly, as being made out of a part of a gown that she and her daughter had bought together in Rochdale.

She stood up, and stretched out her hands in the attitude of blessing over Susan's bent head.

"God bless you, and show you His mercy in your need, as you have shown it to this little child."

She took the little creature in her arms, and smoothed away her sad looks to a smile, and kissed it fondly, saying over and over again, "Nanny, Nanny, my little Nanny." At last the child was soothed, and looked in her face and smiled back again.

"It has her eyes," said she to Susan.

"I never saw her to the best of my knowledge. I think it must be hers by the frock. But where can she be?"

"God knows," said Mrs. Leigh; "I dare not think she's dead. I'm sure she isn't."

"No; she's not dead. Every now and then a little packet is thrust in under our door, with, may be, two half-crowns in it; once it was half-a-sovereign. Altogether I've got seven-and-thirty shillings wrapped up for Nanny. I never touch it, but I've often thought the poor mother feels near to God when she brings this money. Father wanted to set the policeman to watch, but I said No; for I was afraid if she was watched she might not come, and it seemed such a holy thing to he checking her in, I could not find in my heart to do it."

"Oh, if we could but find her! I'd take her in my arms, and we'd just lie down and die together."

"Nay, don't speak so!" said Susan, gently; "for all that's come and gone, she may turn right at last. Mary Magdalen did, you know."

"Eh! but I were nearer right about thee than Will. He thought you would never look on him again if you knew about Lizzie. But thou'rt not a Pharisee."

"I'm sorry he thought I could be so hard," said Susan in a low voice, and colouring up. Then Mrs. Leigh was alarmed, and, in her motherly anxiety, she began to fear lest she had injured Will in Susan's estimation.

"You see Will thinks so much of you--gold would not be good enough for you to walk on, in his eye. He said you'd never look at him as he was, let alone his being brother to my poor wench. He loves you so, it makes him think meanly on everything belonging to himself, as not fit to come near ye; but he's a good lad, and a good son. Thou'lt be a happy woman if thou'lt have him, so don't let my words go against him--don't!"

But Susan hung her head, and made no answer. She had not known until now that Will thought so earnestly and seriously about her; and even now she felt afraid that Mrs. Leigh's words promised her too much happiness, and that they could not be true. At any rate, the instinct of modesty made her shrink from saying anything which might seem like a confession of her own feelings to a third person. Accordingly she turned the conversation on the child.

"I am sure he could not help loving Nanny," said she. "There never was such a good little darling; don't you think she'd win his heart if he knew she was his niece, and perhaps bring him to think kindly on his sister?"

"I dunnot know," said Mrs. Leigh, shaking her head. "He has a turn in his eye like his father, that makes me-- He's right down good though. But you see, I've never been a good one at managing folk; one severe look turns me sick, and then I say just the wrong thing, I'm so fluttered. Now I should like nothing better than to take Nancy home with me, but Tom knows nothing but that his sister is dead, and I've not the knack of speaking rightly to Will. I dare not do it, and that's the truth. But you mun not think badly of Will. He's so good hissel, that he can't understand how any one can do wrong; and, above all, I'm sure he loves you dearly."

"I don't think I could part with Nancy," said Susan, anxious to stop this revelation of Will's attachment to herself. "He'll come round to her soon; he can't fail; and I'll keep a sharp look-out after the poor mother, and try and catch her the next time she comes with her little parcels of money."

"Ay, lass; we mun get hold of her; my Lizzie. I love thee dearly for thy kindness to her child: but, if thou canst catch her for me, I'll pray for thee when I'm too near my death to speak words; and, while I live, I'll serve thee next to her--she mun come first, thou know'st. God bless thee, lass. My heart is lighter by a deal than it was when I comed in. Them lads will be looking for me home, and I mun go, and leave this little sweet one" (kissing it). "If I can take courage, I'll tell Will all that has come and gone between us two. He may come and see thee, mayn't he?"

"Father will be very glad to see him, I'm sure," replied Susan. The way in which this was spoken satisfied Mrs. Leigh's anxious heart that she had done Will no harm by what she had said; and, with many a kiss to the little one, and one more fervent tearful blessing on Susan, she went homewards.

CHAPTER III.

That night Mrs. Leigh stopped at home--that only night for many months. Even Tom, the scholar, looked up from his books in amazement; but then he remembered that Will had not been well, and that his mother's attention having been called to the circumstance, it was only natural she should stay to watch him. And no watching could be more tender, or more complete. Her loving eyes seemed never averted from his face--his grave, sad, careworn face. When Tom went to bed the mother left her seat, and going up to Will, where he sat looking at the fire, but not seeing it, she kissed his forehead, and said--"Will! lad, I've been to see Susan Palmer!"

She felt the start under her hand which was placed on his shoulder, but he was silent for a minute or two. Then he said, -

"What took you there, mother?"

"Why, my lad, it was likely I should wish to see one you cared for; I did not put myself forward. I put on my Sunday clothes, and tried to behave as yo'd ha' liked me. At least, I remember trying at first; but after, I forgot all."

She rather wished that he would question her as to what made her forget all. But he only said -

"How was she looking, mother?"

"Well, thou seest I never set eyes on her before; but she's a good, gentle-looking creature; and I love her dearly, as I've reason to."

Will looked up with momentary surprise, for his mother was too shy to be usually taken with strangers. But, after all, it was naturally in this case, for who could look at Susan without loving her? So still he did not ask any questions, and his poor mother had to take courage, and try again to introduce the subject near to her heart. But how?

"Will!" said she (jerking it out in sudden despair of her own powers to lead to what she wanted to say), "I telled her all."

"Mother! you've ruined me," said he, standing up, and standing opposite to her with a stern white look of affright on his face.

"No! my own dear lad; dunnot look so scared; I have not ruined you!" she exclaimed, placing her two hands on his shoulders, and looking fondly into his face. "She's not one to harden her heart against a mother's sorrow. My own lad, she's too good for that. She's not one to judge and scorn the sinner. She's too deep read in her New Testament for that. Take courage, Will; and thou mayst, for I watched her well, though it is not for one woman to let out another's secret. Sit thee down, lad, for thou look'st very white."

He sat down. His mother drew a stool towards him, and sat at his feet.

"Did you tell her about Lizzie, then?" asked he, hoarse and low.

"I did; I telled her all! and she fell a-crying over my deep sorrow, and the poor wench's sin. And then a light comed into her face, trembling and quivering with some new glad thought; and what dost thou think it was, Will, lad? Nay, I'll not misdoubt but that thy heart will give thanks as mine did, afore God and His angels, for her great goodness. That little Nanny is not her niece, she's our Lizzie's own child, my little grandchild." She could no longer restrain her tears; and they fell hot and fast, but still she looked into his face.

"Did she know it was Lizzie's child? I do not comprehend," said he, flushing red.

"She knows now: she did not at first, but took the little helpless creature in, out of her own pitiful, loving heart, guessing only that it was the child of shame; and she's worked for it, and kept it, and tended it ever sin' it were a mere baby, and loves it fondly. Will! won't you love it?" asked she, beseechingly.

He was silent for an instant; then he said, "Mother, I'll try. Give me time, for all these things startle me. To think of Susan having to do with such a child!"

"Ay, Will! and to think, as may be, yet of Susan having to do with the child's mother! For she is tender and pitiful, and speaks hopefully of my lost one, and will try and find her for me, when she comes, as she does sometimes, to thrust money under the door, for her baby. Think of that, Will. Here's Susan, good and pure as the angels in heaven, yet, like them, full of hope and mercy, and one who, like them, will rejoice over

her as repents. Will, my lad, I'm not afeard of you now; and I must speak, and you must listen. I am your mother, and I dare to command you, because I know I am in the right, and that God is on my side. If He should lead the poor wandering lassie to Susan's door, and she comes back, crying and sorryful, led by that good angel to us once more, thou shalt never say a casting-up word to her about her sin, but be tender and helpful towards one 'who was lost and is found;' so may God's blessing rest on thee, and so mayst thou lead Susan home as thy wife."

She stood no longer as the meek, imploring, gentle mother, but firm and dignified, as if the interpreter of God's will. Her manner was so unusual and solemn, that it overcame all Will's pride and stubbornness. He rose softly while she was speaking, and bent his head, as if in reverence at her words, and the solemn injunction which they conveyed. When she had spoken, he said, in so subdued a voice that she was almost surprised at the sound, "Mother, I will."

"I may be dead and gone; but, all the same, thou wilt take home the wandering sinner, and heal up her sorrows, and lead her to her Father's house. My lad! I can speak no more; I'm turned very faint."

He placed her in a chair; he ran for water. She opened her eyes, and smiled.

"God bless you, Will. Oh! I am so happy. It seems as if she were found; my heart is so filled with gladness."

That night Mr. Palmer stayed out late and long. Susan was afraid that he was at his old haunts and habits--getting tipsy at some public-house; and this thought oppressed her, even though she had so much to make her happy in the consciousness that Will loved her. She sat up long, and then she went to bed, leaving all arranged as well as she could for her father's return. She looked at the little rosy, sleeping girl who was her bed-fellow, with redoubled tenderness, and with many a prayerful thought. The little arms entwined her neck as she lay down, for Nanny was a light sleeper, and was conscious that she, who was loved with all the power of that sweet, childish heart, was near her, and by her, although she was too sleepy to utter any of her half-formed words.

And, by-and-by, she heard her father come home, stumbling uncertain, trying first the windows, and next the door fastenings, with many a loud incoherent murmur. The little innocent twined around her seemed all the sweeter and more lovely, when she thought sadly of her erring father. And presently he called aloud for a light. She had left matches and all arranged as usual on the dresser; but, fearful of some accident from fire, in his unusually intoxicated state, she now got up softly, and putting on a cloak, went down to his assistance.

Alas! the little arms that were unclosed from her soft neck belonged to a light, easily awakened sleeper. Nanny missed her darling Susy; and terrified at being left alone, in the vast mysterious darkness, which had no bounds and seemed infinite, she slipped out of bed, and tottered, in her little nightgown, towards the door. There was a light below, and there was Susy and safety! So she went onwards two steps towards the steep, abrupt stairs; and then, dazzled by sleepiness, she stood, she wavered, she fell! Down on her head on the stone floor she fell! Susan flew to her, and spoke all soft, entreating, loving words; but her white lids covered up the blue violets of eyes, and there was no murmur came out of the pale lips. The warm tears that rained down did not awaken her; she lay stiff, and weary with her short life, on Susan's knee. Susan went sick with terror. She carried her upstairs, and laid her tenderly in bed; she dressed herself most hastily, with her trembling fingers. Her father was asleep on the settle downstairs; and useless, and worse than useless, if awake. But Susan flew out of the door, and down the quiet resounding street, towards the nearest doctor's house. Quickly she went, but as quickly a shadow followed, as if impelled by some sudden terror. Susan rang wildly at the night-bell--the shadow crouched near. The doctor looked out from an upstairs window.

"A little child has fallen downstairs, at No. 9 Crown Street, and is very ill--dying, I'm afraid. Please, for God's sake, sir, come directly. No. 9 Crown Street."

"I'll be there directly," said he, and shut the window.

"For that God you have just spoken about--for His sake--tell me, are you Susan Palmer? Is it my child that lies a-dying?" said the shadow, springing forwards, and clutching poor Susan's arm.

"It is a little child of two years old. I do not know whose it is; I love it as my own. Come with me, whoever you are; come with me."

The two sped along the silent streets--as silent as the night were they. They entered the house; Susan snatched up the light, and carried it upstairs. The other followed.

She stood with wild, glaring eyes by the bedside, never looking at Susan, but hungrily gazing at the little, white, still child. She stooped down, and put her hand tight on her own heart, as if to still its beating, and bent her ear to the pale lips. Whatever the result was, she did not speak; but threw off the bed-clothes wherewith Susan had tenderly covered up the little creature, and felt its left side.

Then she threw up her arms, with a cry of wild despair.

"She is dead! she is dead!"

She looked so fierce, so mad, so haggard, that, for an instant, Susan was terrified; the next, the holy God had put courage into her heart, and her pure arms were round that guilty, wretched creature, and her tears were falling fast and warm upon her breast. But she was thrown off with violence.

"You killed her--you slighted her--you let her fall down those stairs! you killed her!"

Susan cleared off the thick mist before her, and, gazing at the mother with her clear, sweet angel eyes, said, mournfully--"I would have laid down my own life for her."

"Oh, the murder is on my soul!" exclaimed the wild, bereaved mother, with the fierce impetuosity of one who has none to love her, and to be beloved, regard to whom might teach self-restraint.

"Hush!" said Susan, her finger on her lips. "Here is the doctor. God may suffer her to live."

The poor mother turned sharp round. The doctor mounted the stair. Ah! that mother was right; the little child was really dead and gone.

And when he confirmed her judgment, the mother fell down in a fit. Susan, with her deep grief, had to forget herself, and forget her darling (her charge for years), and question the doctor what she must do with the poor wretch, who lay on the floor in such extreme of misery.

"She is the mother!" said she.

"Why did she not take better care of her child?" asked he, almost angrily.

But Susan only said, "The little child slept with me; and it was I that left her."

"I will go back and make up a composing draught; and while I am away you must get her to bed."

Susan took out some of her own clothes, and softly undressed the stiff, powerless form. There was no other bed in the house but the one in which her father slept. So she tenderly lifted the body of her darling; and was going to take it downstairs, but the mother opened her eyes, and seeing what she was about, she said--"I am not worthy to touch her, I am so wicked. I have spoken to you as I never should have spoken; but I think you are very good. May I have my own child to lie in my arms for a little while?"

Her voice was so strange a contrast to what it had been before she had gone into the fit, that Susan hardly recognised it: it was now so unspeakably soft, so irresistibly pleading; the features too had lost their fierce expression, and were almost as placid as death. Susan could not speak, but she carried the little child, and laid it in its mother's arms; then, as she looked at them, something overpowered her, and she knelt down, crying aloud--"Oh, my God, my God, have mercy on her, and forgive and comfort her."

But the mother kept smiling, and stroking the little face, murmuring soft, tender words, as if it were alive. She was going mad, Susan thought; but she prayed on, and on, and ever still she prayed with streaming eyes.

The doctor came with the draught. The mother took it, with docile unconsciousness of its nature as medicine. The doctor sat by her; and soon she fell asleep. Then he rose softly, and beckoning Susan to the door, he spoke to her there.

"You must take the corpse out of her arms. She will not awake. That draught will make her sleep for many hours. I will call before noon again. It is now daylight. Good-by."

Susan shut him out; and then, gently extricating the dead child from its mother's arms, she could not resist making her own quiet moan over her darling. She tried to learn off its little placid face, dumb and pale before her.

Not all the scalding tears of care Shall wash away that vision fair; Not all the thousand thoughts that rise, Not all the sights that dim her eyes, Shall e'er usurp the place Of that little angel-face.

And then she remembered what remained to be done. She saw that all was right in the house; her father was still dead asleep on the settle, in spite of all the noise of the night. She went out through the quiet streets, deserted still, although it was broad daylight, and to where the Leighs lived. Mrs. Leigh, who kept her country hours, was opening her window-shutters. Susan took her by the arm, and, without speaking, went into the house-place. There she knelt down before the astonished Mrs. Leigh, and cried as she had never done before; but the miserable night had overpowered her, and she who had gone through so much calmly, now that the pressure seemed removed could not find the power to speak.

"My poor dear! What has made thy heart so sore as to come and cry a-this-ons? Speak and tell me. Nay, cry on, poor wench, if thou canst not speak yet. It will ease the heart, and then thou canst tell me."

"Nanny is dead!" said Susan. "I left her to go to father, and she fell downstairs, and never breathed again. Oh, that's my sorrow! But I've more to tell. Her mother is come--is in our house! Come and see if it's your Lizzie."

Mrs. Leigh could not speak, but, trembling, put on her things and went with Susan in dizzy haste back to Crown Street.

CHAPTER IV.

As they entered the house in Crown Street, they perceived that the door would not open freely on its hinges, and Susan instinctively looked behind to see the cause of the obstruction. She immediately recognised the appearance of a little parcel, wrapped in a scrap of newspaper, and evidently containing money. She stooped and picked it up. "Look!" said she, sorrowfully, "the mother was bringing this for her child last night."

But Mrs. Leigh did not answer. So near to the ascertaining if it were her lost child or no, she could not be arrested, but pressed onwards with trembling steps and a beating, fluttering heart. She entered the bedroom, dark and still. She took no heed of the little corpse over which Susan paused, but she went straight to the bed, and, withdrawing the curtain, saw Lizzie; but not the former Lizzie, bright, gay, buoyant, and undimmed. This Lizzie was old before her time; her beauty was gone; deep lines of care, and, alas! of want (or thus the mother imagined) were printed on the cheek, so round, and fair, and smooth, when last she gladdened her mother's eyes. Even in her sleep she bore the look of woe and despair which was the prevalent expression of her face by day; even in her sleep she had forgotten how to smile. But all these marks of the sin and sorrow she had passed through only made her mother love her the more. She stood looking at her with greedy eyes, which seemed as though no gazing could satisfy their longing; and at last she stooped down and kissed the pale, worn hand that lay outside the bedclothes. No touch disturbed the sleeper; the mother need not have laid the hand so gently down upon the counterpane. There was no sign of life, save only now and then a deep sob-like sigh. Mrs. Leigh sat down beside the bed, and still holding back the curtain, looked on and on, as if she could never be satisfied.

Susan would fain have stayed by her darling one; but she had many calls upon her time and thoughts, and her will had now, as ever, to be given up to that of others. All seemed to devolve the burden of their cares on her. Her father, ill-humoured from his last night's intemperance, did not scruple to reproach her with being the cause of little Nanny's death; and when, after bearing his upbraiding meekly for some time, she could no longer restrain herself, but began to cry, he wounded her even more by his injudicious attempts at comfort; for he said it was as well the child was dead; it was none of theirs, and why should they be troubled with it?

Susan wrung her hands at this, and came and stood before her father, and implored him to forbear. Then she had to take all requisite steps for the coroner's inquest; she had to arrange for the dismissal of her school; she had to summons a little neighbour, and send his willing feet on a message to William Leigh, who, she felt, ought to be informed of his mother's whereabouts, and of the whole state of affairs. She asked her messenger to tell him to come and speak to her; that his mother was at her house. She was thankful that her father sauntered out to have a gossip at the nearest coach-stand, and to relate as many of the night's adventures as he knew; for as yet he was in ignorance of the watcher and the watched, who silently passed away the hours upstairs.

At dinner-time Will came. He looked red, glad, impatient, excited. Susan stood calm and white before him, her soft, loving eyes gazing straight into his.

"Will," said she, in a low, quiet voice, "your sister is upstairs."

"My sister!" said he, as if affrighted at the idea, and losing his glad look in one of gloom. Susan saw it, and her heart sank a little, but she went on as calm to all appearance as ever.

"She was little Nanny's mother, as perhaps you know. Poor little Nanny was killed last night by a fall downstairs." All the calmness was gone; all the suppressed feeling was displayed in spite of every effort. She sat down, and hid her face from him, and cried bitterly. He forgot everything but the wish, the longing to comfort her. He put his arm round her waist, and bent over her. But all he could say, was, "Oh, Susan, how can I comfort you? Don't take on so--pray don't!" He never changed the words, but the tone varied every time he spoke. At last she seemed to regain her power over herself; and she wiped her eyes, and once more looked upon him with her own quiet, earnest, unfearing gaze.

"Your sister was near the house. She came in on hearing my words to the doctor. She is asleep now, and your mother is watching her. I wanted to tell you all myself. Would you like to see your mother?"

"No!" said he. "I would rather see none but thee. Mother told me thou knew'st all." His eyes were downcast in their shame.

But the holy and pure did not lower or veil her eyes.

She said, "Yes, I know all--all but her sufferings. Think what they must have been!"

He made answer, low and stern, "She deserved them all; every jot."

"In the eye of God, perhaps she does. He is the Judge; we are not."

"Oh!" she said, with a sudden burst, "Will Leigh! I have thought so well of you; don't go and make me think you cruel and hard. Goodness is not goodness unless there is mercy and tenderness with it. There is your mother, who has been nearly heart-broken, now full of rejoicing over her child. Think of your mother."

"I do think of her," said he. "I remember the promise I gave her last night. Thou shouldst give me time. I would do right in time. I never think it o'er in quiet. But I will do what is right and fitting, never fear. Thou hast spoken out very plain to me, and misdoubted me, Susan; I love thee so, that thy words cut me. If I did hang back a bit from making sudden promises, it was because not even for love of thee, would I say what I was not feeling; and at first I could not feel all at once as thou wouldst have me. But I'm not cruel and hard; for if I had been, I should na' have grieved as I have done."

He made as if he were going away; and indeed he did feel he would rather think it over in quiet. But Susan, grieved at her incautious words, which had all the appearance of harshness, went a step or two nearer-- paused--and then, all over blushes, said in a low, soft whisper -

"Oh, Will! I beg your pardon. I am very sorry. Won't you forgive me?"

She who had always drawn back, and been so reserved, said this in the very softest manner; with eyes now uplifted beseechingly, now dropped to the ground. Her sweet confusion told more than words could do; and Will turned back, all joyous in his certainty of being beloved, and took her in his arms, and kissed her.

"My own Susan!" he said.

Meanwhile the mother watched her child in the room above.

It was late in the afternoon before she awoke, for the sleeping draught had been very powerful. The instant she awoke, her eyes were fixed on her mother's face with a gaze as unflinching as if she were fascinated.

Mrs. Leigh did not turn away, nor move; for it seemed as if motion would unlock the stony command over herself which, while so perfectly still, she was enabled to preserve. But by-and-by Lizzie cried out, in a piercing voice of agony -

"Mother, don't look at me! I have been so wicked!" and instantly she hid her face, and grovelled among the bed-clothes, and lay like one dead, so motionless was she.

Mrs. Leigh knelt down by the bed, and spoke in the most soothing tones.

"Lizzie, dear, don't speak so. I'm thy mother, darling; don't be afeard of me. I never left off loving thee, Lizzie. I was always a- thinking of thee. Thy father forgave thee afore he died." (There was a little start here, but no sound was heard.) "Lizzie, lass, I'll do aught for thee; I'll live for thee; only don't be afeard of me. Whate'er thou art or hast been, we'll ne'er speak on't. We'll leave th' oud times behind us, and go back to the Upclose Farm. I but left it to find thee, my lass; and God has led me to thee. Blessed be His name. And God is good, too, Lizzie. Thou hast not forgot thy Bible, I'll be bound, for thou wert always a scholar. I'm no reader, but I learnt off them texts to comfort me a bit, and I've said them many a time a day to myself. Lizzie, lass, don't hide thy head so; it's thy mother as is speaking to thee. Thy little child clung to me only yesterday; and if it's gone to be an angel, it will speak to God for thee. Nay, don't sob a that 'as; thou shalt have it again in heaven; I know thou'lt strive to get there, for thy little Nancy's sake--and listen! I'll tell thee God's promises to them that are penitent--only doan't be afeard."

Mrs. Leigh folded her hands, and strove to speak very clearly, while she repeated every tender and merciful text she could remember. She could tell from the breathing that her daughter was listening; but she was so dizzy and sick herself when she had ended, that she could not go on speaking. It was all she could do to keep from crying aloud.

At last she heard her daughter's voice.

"Where have they taken her to?" she asked.

"She is downstairs. So quiet, and peaceful, and happy she looks."

"Could she speak! Oh, if God--if I might but have heard her little voice! Mother, I used to dream of it. May I see her once again? Oh, mother, if I strive very hard and God is very merciful, and I go to heaven, I shall not know her--I shall not know my own again: she will shun me as a stranger, and chug to Susan Palmer and to you. Oh, woe! Oh, woe!" She shook with exceeding sorrow.

In her earnestness of speech she had uncovered her face, and tried to read Mrs. Leigh's thoughts through her looks. And when she saw those aged eyes brimming full of tears, and marked the quivering lips, she threw her arms round the faithful mother's neck, and wept there, as she had done in many a childish sorrow, but with a deeper, a more wretched grief.

Her mother hushed her on her breast; and lulled her as if she were a baby; and she grew still and quiet.

They sat thus for a long, long time. At last, Susan Palmer came up with some tea and bread and butter for Mrs. Leigh. She watched the mother feed her sick, unwilling child, with every fond inducement to eat which she could devise; they neither of them took notice of Susan's presence. That night they lay in each other's arms; but Susan slept on the ground beside them.

They took the little corpse (the little unconscious sacrifice, whose early calling-home had reclaimed her poor wandering mother) to the hills, which in her life-time she had never seen. They dared not lay her by the stern grandfather in Milne Row churchyard, but they bore her to a lone moorland graveyard, where, long ago, the Quakers used to bury their dead. They laid her there on the sunny slope, where the earliest spring flowers blow.

Will and Susan live at the Upclose Farm. Mrs. Leigh and Lizzie dwell in a cottage so secluded that, until you drop into the very hollow where it is placed, you do not see it. Tom is a schoolmaster in Rochdale, and he and Will help to support their mother. I only know that, if the cottage be hidden in a green hollow of the hills, every sound of sorrow in the whole upland is heard there--every call of suffering or of sickness for help is listened to by a sad, gentle- looking woman, who rarely smiles (and when

Why still haven't broken free.

she does her smile is more sad than other people's tears), but who comes out of her seclusion whenever there is a shadow in any household. Many hearts bless Lizzie Leigh, but she--she prays always and ever for forgiveness-- such forgiveness as may enable her to see her child once more. Mrs. Leigh is quiet and happy. Lizzie is, to her eyes, something precious--as the lost piece of silver--found once more. Susan is the bright one who brings sunshine to all. Children grow around her and call her blessed. One is called Nanny; her Lizzie often takes to the sunny graveyard in the uplands, and while the little creature gathers the daisies, and makes chains, Lizzie sits by a little grave and weeps bitterly.

25165641R00020

Printed in Great Britain
by Amazon